THE OFFICIAL
TRIVIA & QUIZ BOOK

By Emma Harrison

Based on the series created by Michael Poryes and Rich Correll & Barry O'Brien

NEW YORK
AN IMPRINT OF DISNEY BOOK GROUP

Printed in the United States of America

First Edition
1 3 5 7 9 10 8 6 4 2

Library of Congress Control Number on file.
ISBN 978-1-4231-1063-7

For more Disney Press fun, visit www.disneybooks.com
Visit DisneyChannel.com

You've watched every episode of *Hannah Montana* roughly 615 times. You know all the words to "I've Got Nerve." (You can even recite them backward!) You've created your own special dance to "Best of Both Worlds." Maybe you've even sat front row, center at one of Hannah's rockin' concerts.

But are you a true *Hannah Montana* fan? How much do you *really* know about our favorite double-life-leading pop star and her cool friends and family? Well, you're about to find out—just take the fun quizzes in this book to test your knowledge about your fave TV show.

And don't forget to check out the tons of personality quizzes in the book as well! They'll reveal different sides of your personality, test how you'd react in challenging situations, and show how well you'd fit into Hannah's world.

Sweet niblets, what are you waiting for? Grab a pencil and get started!

Hannah Montana Trivia Quiz #1: Take the Stage

When Hannah hits the stage to perform at another sold-out concert, she gives it her all. And we know you'll do the same as you take the six Hannah Montana trivia quizzes in this book! Think of this first quiz as your opening number—we know you'll have us cheering! But be warned: each quiz is tougher than the last as we test your knowledge of all things Hannah.

1. **What are the first names of Miley's brother and father?**
   - A. Jordan and Robby
   - B. Jackson and Robby
   - C. Jack and Billy

2. **Who is the first friend Miley tells about her big Hannah Montana secret?**
   - A. Oliver
   - B. Amber
   - C. Lilly

3. **What do Miley and her brother call their grandmother?**
   - A. Ma'maw
   - B. Grandma
   - C. Bubbe

4. **Miley's first kiss is shared with which of the following characters?**
   - A. Oliver
   - B. Jake
   - C. Josh

5. **What career did Miley's dad have before he became Hannah's manager?**
   - A. He was a singer.
   - B. He was a teacher.
   - C. He was an actor.

6. **Which team do Miley and Lilly try out for together?**
   - A. Basketball
   - B. Track
   - C. Cheerleading

7. What name does Lilly use when she goes undercover as Hannah Montana's best friend?

A. Lala
B. Lola
C. Lavender

8. In the first season of *Hannah Montana*, why does Miley almost tell a reporter about her secret identity?

A. She wants to be more famous.
B. She's irritated about Jake Ryan getting treated like a star at school and wishes she could get special treatment, too.
C. She wants to give the reporter a scoop.

ANSWERS:

1. B   5. A
2. C   6. C
3. A   7. B
4. B   8. B

SCORING:

Give yourself two points
for each correct answer.

If you scored:

0–4
Hannah Novice

Have you ever seen an episode of
Hannah Montana? We're not so
sure. Maybe you're watching some
other undercover pop-star show.

6–10
Hannah Apprentice

You've got your basic Hannah
facts down, but you're not quite
an expert yet. Better watch a few
more episodes before moving on
to Hannah Montana Trivia Quiz #2.

12–16
Hannah Master

You've certainly been paying
attention to the universe
of Hannah Montana. (The
Hannahverse?) Congratulations!
We can't wait to see how you'll do
on the next quiz!

What's Your Hannah Montana Style?

Every girl should have her own personal style. Well, unless you're Miley Stewart, and then you have two personal styles—one for you and one for your superstar other half, Hannah Montana. Miley's wardrobe is all sweet, school-girl cool, while Hannah's is trendy, flashy, and pop-star sleek. And let's not forget Lilly Truscott, a girl with a funky, tomboyish fashion sense like no other. Take this quiz and find out which Hannah Montana style is right for you!

1. **It's the first day of school and you've laid out all your new school clothes on your bed so that you can choose the perfect outfit. Your bed is overflowing with:**
   A. Colorful shorts and T-shirts, plus tons of funky hats and accessories.
   B. Pretty skirts, dresses, and tanks in pastels and bright colors.
   C. Trendy jeans, embellished jackets, flashy scarves, and supercool shades.

2. **If a fashion photographer came by to take a picture of your closet, what would she find?**
   A. A mess of jeans, sneakers, flip-flops, and T-shirts
   B. A neatly organized closet with everything separated by season and filled with fun, casual clothes
   C. A brightly lit walk-in closet packed with all the latest styles

3. **Your parents are making you wear a plain black dress to a neighborhood party. You simply cannot imagine looking so blah—after all, it *is* a party!—so you accessorize the dress with:**

    A. A sideways cabbie hat and a macramé bracelet.

    B. A delicate necklace and cute purse.

    C. A sequined scarf, twenty bracelets, and gold platform sandals.

4. **You've just won backstage passes to the Justin Timberlake concert. Tons of famous people are going to be there. What do you wear?**

    A. Your lucky sneakers. Maybe you can convince some celebs to autograph them.

    B. Something pretty but not too flashy. You're not about snagging the spotlight.

    C. An outfit ripped from the pages of *CosmoGirl*. Gotta look good for the press!

5. **Time for a day at the beach! What's the most important fashion accessory for you to bring along?**

    A. A wet suit so you can hit the waves, baby!

    B. Those cute new flip-flops with the flowers all over them.

    C. Big sunglasses, a wide-brimmed hat, and a fashion magazine that you can either read or use to hide behind when the paparazzi approach.

6. **There's a pirate-themed dance at school and you know your crush is going to be there. What do you wear?**

    A. Pirate shirt, eye patch, peg leg, head bandana. You take theme dances very seriously.

    B. A sleek new dress. And maybe a temporary skull-and-crossbones tattoo just to show you're in the spirit.

    C. A dramatic dress that looks something like what Keira Knightley wore in *Pirates of the Caribbean*. So now.

7. Finish this sentence: "My perfect hairstyle is":
  A. Anything that will keep it out of my face.
  B. Something soft, natural, and timeless.
  C. Sleek, highlighted, and of the moment.

8. What's the one fashion accessory you're never seen without?
  A. Your skateboard
  B. Your backpack
  C. Your wig

9. When it comes to patterns, you prefer:
  A. Plaid, argyle, and maybe some camouflage.
  B. Florals and stripes.
  C. Patterns? Forget patterns. Give me sequins!

SCORING:

Mostly A's:
You are LILLY TRUSCOTT!

You're fun, active, and always ready for an adventure, so your clothes have to be ready for one, too! Whether you're at the beach, hanging at school, or boarding with your buddies, your fashion choices fit right in with your lifestyle—funky, colorful, and flexible.

Mostly B's:
You are MILEY STEWART!

Sweet and feminine, your clothes tell the world that you're a nice, casual girl who's easygoing and approachable. You prefer flirty over flashy, and you're a laid-back person who knows how to have a little fun.

Mostly C's:
You are HANNAH MONTANA!

You wannabe rock star, you! Your trendy outfits are the envy of every girl at every fabulous party you attend. With your flashy accessories and five-minutes-from-now hairstyles, you're always ready to strike a pose.

Did You Know?

Miley Cyrus already had the part of Hannah Montana when Emily Osment auditioned for the role of Lilly. The two of them totally clicked, and it was clear they were meant to play best friends!

Are You a Loyal Friend?

Miley and Lilly have been through a lot. First, their friendship was tested big-time when Lilly found out that Miley had been keeping the most major secret of all time— she was pop star Hannah Montana. Then, Lilly made the cheerleading squad and Miley didn't, and after that they both started crushing on the same boy. . . .

But through all their ups and downs, Miley and Lilly always find a way to stick by each other. Would you do the same for your BFF? Take this quiz and find out!

ı. **You've been dying to see a new movie, and your best friend has promised to go with you on opening night. Then she finds out that the movie opens on the same night as the school concert— and she's scheduled to play a piano solo! You:**

  A. Wish her luck and go to the movie on your own. After all, you've been talking about nothing else for months—how can you wait another minute to see this flick?

  B. Skip the movie and go to her concert. The flick will still be playing tomorrow.

  C. Go to the concert, but leave right after her solo to catch a late showing of the movie.

2. **You score two tickets to a concert being given by your best friend's favorite band. Problem? It's also your crush's favorite band, and this is the perfect opportunity to ask him out. You:**
   A. Talk to your friend and see how she'd feel about you asking your crush. (You're sure she'll understand.)
   B. Ask the boy. You've been waiting for a chance like this forever!
   C. Take your best friend. You've known her your whole life and you've known your crush for a month.

3. **The popular kids ask you to sit with them at lunch. If you go, you'll be leaving your BFF alone. You:**
   A. Say, "No thanks."
   B. Tell your friend it's just for one day and hope she understands.
   C. Sit with them. Hesitation is not an option. They may take back the invite.

4. **You and your best friend both try out for the softball team. She makes varsity and you make junior varsity. You:**
   A. Play on the JV team and make some new friends.
   B. Try to go to as many of her games as you can and ask her to help you improve your skills. Maybe you'll get bumped up to varsity!
   C. Quit the team and give her the cold shoulder. She should have offered to quit as soon as she knew you wouldn't be together.

5. **Your BFF runs up to you and tells you that she has a crush on the new boy in school. Bummer. You were about to tell her that you have a crush on the same boy. You:**
   A. Say nothing, but try to win him behind her back. If he chooses you, it's not your fault.
   B. Tell her the truth and try to figure something out, but vow to each other never to let a boy come between you.
   C. Bite your tongue and ignore the guy from that second on. She got there first.

SCORING:

If you scored:

0-3
With Friends Like You, Who Needs Enemies?

Is this girl really your best friend or are you only out for number one? If you want to keep your BFF around, we suggest you start thinking about her every once in a while. Otherwise, you might soon find yourself friend-free.

4-7
A Little for You, a Little for Her

You're a good friend, but you also know how to take care of yourself when it's really important. That's not a bad thing as long as you make sure you think of other people's feelings as you're making your decisions. Who knows? You may be able to get what you want *and* keep your friends happy at the same time.

8-10
That's What Friends Are For!

You are the *best* best friend a girl could ask for. You step aside when you're crushing on the same boy, and you put all her wants and needs ahead of your own. But wait— what about what *you* want? Make sure you're not giving up the things you want just to please her. Otherwise, you might end up hurt, and that's not good for either of you!

Could You Lead a Double Life?

Being Hannah Montana is tough. It really is! Miley has to watch every thing she says and does to make sure she doesn't give away her secret. One mistake and her double life is done! Take our quiz to find out if you could lead a double life like Miley!

1. **Your best friend told you about her new crush and made you _swear_ you wouldn't tell a soul. How long did it take you to spill the beans?**
   - A. About five minutes. You have no control over your tongue.
   - B. A few weeks, but the person who you told was really grilling you!
   - C. It's been years, and you still haven't told.

2. **None of your tomboy friends knows that you take ballet classes every Saturday. You're hanging out with them in the park when a girl from your ballet class approaches. You:**
   - A. Casually walk over to her so you can chat out of earshot of your friends.
   - B. Talk to her when she comes over, trying desperately to steer the conversation away from all things ballet.
   - C. Give up and tell your friends everything, hoping they'll accept that a person can have a lot of different interests.

3. **You promised your best friend you wouldn't buy that same pink tank top she got for her birthday, but it was so cute you couldn't resist. All you've got to do is wear it when she won't see you. You:**
   - A. Wear it to school months after you buy it.
   - B. Wear it to school the day after you buy it. You totally forgot it was supposed to be a secret shirt.
   - C. Still haven't worn it in her presence.

4. **When it comes to organizing your schedule and getting to clubs and games and parties on time, you are:**
   A. Perfect. Never late. Always know where you need to be.
   B. Awful. You're always showing up for basketball on days you're supposed to be at Model U.N.
   C. Okay. There have been a few late arrivals and slipups, but nothing major.

5. **Your father tells you that he might, *might*, be able to get you and all your friends into Six Flags for free this weekend but not to tell anyone until it's a done deal. You:**
   A. Keep your mouth shut. You don't want to promise something you can't deliver.
   B. Tell everyone. You can't keep something that exciting to yourself.
   C. Tell only your best friend but warn her that it may not happen.

6. **Your friends from cheerleading show up at your house to kidnap you for a pancake breakfast. Surprise! You have exactly five minutes to get ready.**
   A. You trip as you run up the stairs, sprain your ankle, and have to stay at home with an ice pack.
   B. You're dressed in four minutes flat. Not only that, you look fabulous.
   C. You end up wearing an okay outfit, but you're a little sweaty from rushing to dress, and your hair . . . well, baseball caps were made for a reason.

SCORING:

1. A-0, B-1, C-2
2. A-2, B-1, C-0
3. A-1, B-0, C-2
4. A-2, B-0, C-1
5. A-2, B-0, C-1
6. A-0, B-2, C-1

Did You Know?

Before she could even talk, Miley Cyrus knew the song "Hound Dog" and would sing it with her dad.

If you scored:

0–4
One Life to Live

So keeping a secret is not your best talent. You weren't meant to lead a double life, but that's okay—it looks like you might have your hands full with the one you've got!

5–8
Double Duty, Maybe

You've got some skills in deception. We bet you could get away with having a second life, for a little while anyway.

9–12
Secret Agent Girl!

Wow! You keep secrets in the vault, know how to handle uncomfortable situations with ease, and can do a quick change even faster than Hannah. Wait. Are you really you right now, or are you someone else?

Hannah Montana Trivia Quiz #2: Pumpin' Up the Party

So you totally rocked the first quiz, huh? Feeling like you can do no wrong where *Hannah Montana* trivia is concerned? Good for you! We like your confidence. But we're kicking it up a notch with this quiz, so let's see how you do on these slightly tougher Hannah questions.

1. When Hannah guest starred on Jake's TV show, *Zombie High*, what was the name of the character she played?
    A. Miranda, Princess of the Undead
    B. Zaranda, Princess of the Undead
    C. Hannah, Princess of the Undead

2. In order to make Jake jealous, Miley flirts with a boy who she thinks is a senior. What's the boy's name?
    A. Walter
    B. Warren
    C. Willis

3. What grade is the boy she flirts with actually in?
    A. Tenth
    B. Ninth
    C. Eighth

4. Which of the following international VIPs does Hannah perform a private concert for?
    A. The Queen of England and her daughter
    B. The King of Spain and his daughter
    C. The Queen of France and her daughter

5. When Jackson tricks Miley into babysitting for Mr. Dontzig's niece, she ends up taking the girl to a toy store to make a stuffed _____?
    A. Bear
    B. Moose
    C. Donkey

6. **When Robby gets the flu, which character comes over to the house to take care of him?**

   A. Roxy, Hannah's bodyguard

   B. Mr. Dontzig, the Stewarts' neighbor

   C. Ma'maw, Robby's mom

7. **What's the name of Miley and Jackson's aunt, who comes to visit and causes some problems with her video camera?**

   A. Molly

   B. Ronnie

   C. Dolly

8. **When Miley tries out for the cheerleading squad, she ends up getting the mascot job. What's the mascot of Seaview High School?**

   A. A cowboy

   B. A pirate

   C. A bear

ANSWERS:

1. B   5. B
2. C   6. A
3. C   7. C
4. A   8. B

SCORING:

Give yourself two points for each correct answer.

If you scored:

0–4
"Nobody's Perfect"

Okay, so you made some mistakes. Well, more than a few. But that's okay. As Hannah's song says, "Nobody's perfect." Keep watching the show, and we're sure you'll be hitting high notes in no time!

6–10
"Make Some Noise"

Can you hear the crowd cheering for you? That's because you did a fab job! You clearly know a lot about Miley and her friends!

12–16
"This Is the Life"

Kick back and enjoy the moment, because this is the life! You are a *Hannah Montana* whiz!

Which *Hannah Montana* Character Are You?

Are you a sweet girl with a sassy side like Miley/Hannah? A jokester tomboy like Lilly? Or a prankster and schemer like Jackson? Who knows? Well, we do! Or we will, once you take our *Hannah Montana* personality quiz!

1. Your crush is hanging out at a table in the mall. You stroll by trying to look cool but end up tripping and falling right on your face. He and his friends all crack up laughing. You:

    A. Blush, stammer something silly, and run.

    B. Challenge them all to an arm-wrestling contest. They'll forget your humiliation when you take them down, one by one!

    C. Tell them you meant to do that, just to give them a laugh.

2. Your parents ground you on the night of the big homecoming dance. What do you do?

    A. Sit around watching TV and wait to hear all the details from your best friend.

    B. Set up an obstacle course in your basement and make your own fun.

    C. Sneak out of the house, leaving twenty stuffed animals in your bed to look as if you are there.

3. What's your favorite way to kill time?

    A. Doing something artistic like singing, writing, or drawing

    B. Doing something athletic like swimming, boarding, or surfing

    C. Doing something that will make you some cash

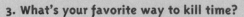

Miley Cyrus and
Emily Osment are
good friends even
off the set.

4. **Your best friend just got dumped by her boyfriend and needs some cheering up. What do you do?**

    A. Go to her house with ice cream and settle in for a nice, long talk.

    B. Get her out of the house to go in-line skating near the beach. Sun, fun, and major endorphins are the best remedies for heartbreak.

    C. Figure out a creative way to get back at the guy.

5. **During gym class, two captains are picking teams for soccer. You're sure to be picked:**

    A. Last. You're not much of an athlete.

    B. First. Gym is your thing.

    C. Somewhere in the middle. Usually you're good at sports, but everyone knows you're easily distracted, and you've been known to take a ball to the face now and then.

6. **Three days ago your parents gave you a list of five chores you need to complete in order to get your allowance. What happened to the list?**

    A. You completed all the chores. You know you have to earn your allowance.

    B. Darn. Between the surf tournament and your lacrosse game you forgot all about that list.

    C. You're putting it off for as long as possible, but you'll do it eventually. You need the cash!

SCORING:

Mostly A's
You are MILEY/HANNAH!
Sweet, responsible, and creative, you're a good friend and a good daughter. And, okay, maybe you're not great at sports, but you try your best. You're a whiz at keeping secrets and a great listener. Congrats on being the kind of girl a friend can really trust.

Mostly B's
You are LILLY!
Fun, energetic, and spontaneous, you definitely know how to have a nonstop good time. You can be a little scatterbrained at times, but that's just because you have so much going on. Plus you're always there for your friends.

Mostly C's
You are JACKSON!
Always got a scheme up your sleeve? Yeah. We thought so. There's never a dull moment when you're around because you always spice things up with a wacky joke or a crazy plot. You can usually be trusted to party now and work later. But at least you do get your work done. Eventually.

Is Your Crush Crushing Back?

Being a teen pop sensation has a lot of perks. You get fabulous clothes, millions of adoring fans, incredible trips all over the world. . . . But even when you're a superstar, boys are still totally confusing.

Just ask Hannah Montana. She may have the music world totally wired, but when it comes to guys, she's just as clueless as the rest of us. How is a girl supposed to know if a guy is crushing on her or not? Try taking our quiz to find out whether the boy of your dreams is dreaming about you, too.

1. **At lunch you snag your crush's phone to check out his ringtones and just happen to notice his speed-dial list. Where are you on the list?**
    - A. #1 or #2
    - B. #9 (the last one)
    - C. You aren't on it.

2. **This morning the homecoming court was announced, and you were nominated for homecoming queen! After homeroom you see your crush in the hallway. He:**
    - A. Nods hello and keeps walking.
    - B. Congratulates you on making the cut.
    - C. Tells you he always knew you'd be homecoming queen (even though you haven't won yet) and that he's already saved up tux money for the dance, in case, you know, he needs it.

3. **You landed the solo at the recent choral concert and invited all your friends, including your crush. Did he show?**
   - A. Yes! And he sat in the front row and gave you a standing ovation.
   - B. Yes, but he was late and had to take a seat in the back.
   - C. No. He had some new video game he wanted to conquer.

4. **Everyone in chemistry class has to pick partners for the monthly lab project. You immediately turn to your crush. He:**
   - A. Says he's sorry, but he promised one of his buddies that they'd work together this time around. He adds that he'll definitely partner with you on next month's project.
   - B. Is looking right at you—as soon as the teacher announced that it was time to pick partners, he turned to you.
   - C. Is already firing up the Bunsen burner with someone else.

5. **You're exhausted after a day at the beach and can't wait to get home and shower. Then you discover that someone stole your bike! Luckily, your crush is right there, unlocking his bike. You tell him what happened. He:**
   - A. Offers you a ride home on his handlebars, stays with you while you call the police to report the theft, and buys you an ice-cream cone to cheer you up.
   - B. Says, "That stinks" and rides off.
   - C. Lets you borrow his cell phone to call your parents for a ride, then heads off to meet his buddies.

ANSWERS:

If you scored:

0-3
The Friend Zone

We're sure your crush has many great qualities, but it seems like he's only interested in you as a friend. The good news? There are plenty of guys out there who will be more concerned with your feelings. It's time to move on to someone worthy of your attention.

4-7
Mixed-Signal Station

Wow! Your guy must really be confusing you. One day he's flirting, and the next day it's like you don't even exist. Maybe he needs a little nudge to help him wake up. Tell him you want to hang out on your own—just the two of you—and see what happens.

8-10
Crush City!

Congratulations! This boy is crushing on you big-time. If he hasn't told you how he feels yet, it might be because he's nervous you don't feel the same. Sooner or later one of you is going to have to step up and confess your crush! Be brave and go for it. We hope you live happily ever after.

Do You "Got Nerve"?

One of Hannah's most popular songs is all about being brave and making the most of your life. For some people, bravery comes naturally. For most of us, it's pretty tough! But taking a leap and doing things that make us uncomfortable is usually very rewarding. Take our quiz and find out if you've got what it takes to step out of your comfort zone!

1. **You and your BFF are hanging out at the mall when you spot a group of cute boys from another school. One of them in particular is smiling in your direction. What do you do?**
   A. Flip your hair, try to look cute, and hope he comes over.
   B. Walk over to him and introduce yourself.
   C. Grab your friend's hand and duck into a store to watch him through the window until he walks away.

2. **It's oral-book-report day in English class. Your teacher asks for someone to volunteer to go first. You:**
   A. Raise your hand. Your report is good, and once you're done you get to sit back and relax.
   B. Wait for someone else to volunteer. You'll raise your hand later, once you've seen how other people do.
   C. Hide behind your book and pray there's a fire drill before you're called on.

3. **You've been standing in line at the ice-cream parlor forever. Just as you get to the counter, a tough-looking girl cuts right in front of you. You:**
   - A. Tell her (politely) that you think you were next.
   - B. Swallow nervously and let it go.
   - C. Step right in front of her and order your ice cream.

4. **There's a dance marathon at your school with all proceeds going to charity. All your friends are going to take part, but there's just one problem—you're a terrible dancer. You:**
   - A. Sign up anyway. Who cares if you look a little silly? It's for charity!
   - B. Make a donation and sit in the bleachers to watch.
   - C. Give it a try, but fake a twisted ankle after the first ten minutes. You feel too self-conscious to stick with it.

5. **The French Club has decided to set up a dunking booth at the spring carnival. Now they just need five people to volunteer to be dunked. You:**
   - A. Are the first to sign up. Could be fun!
   - B. Creep to the back of the crowd. No way you're sitting up there in a bathing suit in front of the entire school.
   - C. Say you'll sit in the dunking booth, but only if they don't get enough people.

6. **Someone drew a moustache on the photo of your principal in the main office. The vice principal storms into your homeroom and calls out one of the boys, saying he knows he's the culprit. Problem? You saw another boy in your class doing the artwork. You:**

   A. Say nothing. After all, if people are innocent, they have nothing to fear, right?

   B. Speak right up and tell the V.P. he has the wrong man, then point out the bad guy.

   C. Wait until after class, then go to the office to tell the V.P.—in private—what you saw.

7. **It's class-picture day. You sit on the stool and give your best smile but blink when the flash goes off. The photographer is already shouting for the next person in line. You:**

   A. Slink off and hope for the best.

   B. Tell the photographer you blinked and demand he take another shot.

   C. Try to sneak a peek at his computer. If your pic is bad, get back in line, wait your turn, and beg the photographer to give you another chance.

ANSWERS:

1. A-1, B-2, C-0   5. A-2, B-0, C-1
2. A-2, B-1, C-0   6. A-0, B-2, C-1
3. A-1, B-0, C-2   7. A-0, B-2, C-1
4. A-2, B-0, C-1

If you scored:

0–4
Quaking in Your Boots

Ever hear the expression "the risk is worth the reward?" Yeah. We didn't think so. Okay, maybe you're naturally shy, but if you don't come out of your shell once in a while, the world is going to pass you by!

5–9
Cautiously Adventurous

You're a risk taker . . . sometimes. You'll try new things as long as they don't look too dangerous, and you'll speak up as long as you won't get hurt. If you keep thinking things through, you should have a fun-filled and injury-free life!

10–14
You've Got Nerve!

Well, well, you certainly are a brave girl! Maybe a little bit too brave. We admire your willingness to try absolutely anything, but you've got to look before you leap every once in a while or you might get hurt.

Which *Hannah Montana* Guy Is Right for You?

Miley has some of the coolest guys ever in her life! Talented and handsome Jake Ryan, sweet and funny Oliver Oken, wacky and adventurous Jackson Stewart...well, all right, Jackson's her brother and sometimes he annoys her, but we think he's totally crush-worthy. Take our quiz to find out which *Hannah Montana* guy is right for you.

1. Close your eyes and imagine your perfect first date. Which of these options comes closest to what you imagined?

A. Grabbing a burger at the beach and then catching some waves before having ice cream for dessert

B. Going for a drive to an out-of-the-way restaurant, then doing something either unexpectedly cool, like salsa dancing, or outrageously offbeat, like miniature golf

C. Taking in a fabulous show (maybe even a movie premiere), then dancing the night away at the hottest club in town

2. **Any guy I go out with has to be:**
   - A. Funny and sweet.
   - B. Up for anything, no matter how crazy.
   - C. Gorgeous.

3. **It's Valentine's Day and your sweetie has given you the most perfect gift ever. What is it?**
   - A. A homemade valentine that tells you how he really feels
   - B. A foolproof escape plan for sneaking out of your house after curfew
   - C. A dozen roses and a fabulous necklace

4. **Your perfect guy has an article written about him in the local paper. What's the headline?**
   - A. Local High Schooler Steals Spotlight as Student Talent Show MC!
   - B. Local High Schooler Impersonates Security Guard to Help Friends Sneak into Rock Concert!
   - C. Meet the Hottest Teen Star in the Universe!

5. **You just received a D on a big history test and have to write a paper to make up for the grade. Your perfect boy would cheer you up by:**
   - A. Keeping you supplied with sodas and snacks as you work on your paper.
   - B. Cracking jokes and making you laugh as you work.
   - C. Looking deeply into your eyes and telling you he knows you can do it.

6. **Which of the following magazines would your perfect boy subscribe to?**
   - A. *Surfing*
   - B. *Mad*
   - C. *Entertainment Weekly*

7. You're walking down the street with your friends and your perfect boy drives by. What kind of car is he riding in?

    A. Car? What car? He rides a bike. Everywhere.

    B. A vintage convertible. Well, it's a bit of a clunker—but still cool!

    C. A limo, naturally.

8. The class clown bets your perfect man twenty bucks that he would never dress like a girl, stand in front of the class, and recite poetry. Your man:

    A. Says, "You're right. I could never do that. Poetry gives me stage fright."

    B. Is in a dress and spouting rhymes before you can blink. Twenty bucks is twenty bucks!

    C. Has no problem playing any part, no matter how silly. After all, he's a professional actor.

SCORING:

Mostly A's:

Your perfect Hannah Montana guy is OLIVER OKEN!

Looking for a sweet guy who's not only very attentive, but can also make you laugh? You've found him in Oliver. He's not just a good guy, but a good friend. What more could you ask for?

Mostly B's:

Your perfect Hannah Montana guy is JACKSON STEWART!

Not only can Jackson help you get out of that fifth-period quiz, he's also supercreative, thoughtful, and knows how to keep you guessing. Life with Jackson Stewart will never be boring!

Mostly C's:

Your perfect Hannah Montana guy is JAKE RYAN!

So cool he's hot, Jake Ryan is every girl's dream. He's gorgeous, sophisticated, and can take you to all those exclusive Hollywood parties. Better start practicing your red-carpet smile!

Hannah Montana Trivia Quiz #3
In the Groove

So you've got the party going by acing the first two quizzes in style. Nice job! But you've got a few more quizzes to complete before you get to take your final bow. So kick out the jams and rock this quiz—after all, you're in the groove now!

1. What is the name of Mr. Dontzig's nightmare niece whom Miley is forced to babysit for?

    A. Patty

    B. Jenny

    C. Penny

2. According to a professional who visits the Stewart home, Jackson has "the gift" for which of the following careers?

    A. Musician

    B. Plumber

    C. Carpenter

3. While dressed up as the Seaview pirate at a basketball game, Miley gets into a fight with another mascot. What kind of animal is the mascot she fights with?

    A. An eagle

    B. A flamingo

    C. A tiger

4. What's the name of Robby Ray's former agent?

    A. Micky Carter

    B. Mike Star

    C. Marty Klein

5. Lilly loses her contacts right before what important event? (Hint: she ends up having to wear her glasses instead.)

    A. The big dance

    B. The half-pipe finals

    C. Her first game as a cheerleader

6. Which of the following gross habits is a particular pet peeve of Oliver's?

    A. Gum chewing

    B. Burping

    C. Nail-biting

7. In the very first *Hannah Montana* episode, Miley spills something all over herself while checking out a boy and then has to pretend it's moisturizer. What does she spill on herself?

    A. Mayonnaise

    B. Whipped cream

    C. Ketchup

8. Which of the following *High School Musical* stars has guest-starred on *Hannah Montana*?

    A. Corbin Bleu

    B. Ashley Tisdale

    C. Both

    D. Neither

ANSWERS:

1. A
2. B
3. B
4. C
5. B
6. A
7. C
8. C

SCORING:

Give yourself two points for each correct answer.

If you scored:

0–4
Backup Singer

Well, you gave it your best try, but our brain stumpers stumped you. That's okay—you can sing in the background until you're ready to take center stage. We know you can do it next time!

6–10
Singing Harmony

Good job. You know your Hannah trivia very well. You may not be quite ready to be the star attraction, but you can support her in style—and if you watch a few more episodes, we know you'll be ready to grab the mic and belt out a solo in style!

12–16
Headline Act

Wow, Hannah genius, there seems to be nothing you don't know about *Hannah Montana*. You're more than ready to stand in the spotlight. In fact, we're surprised you're not there right now!

Can You Keep a Secret?

Miley has a huge secret. Every day she has to act like she's not Hannah Montana. We'd want to shout that news from every rooftop in town, but Miley's committed to having a normal life. For a long time she didn't tell anyone her secret, but she finally decided she could trust Lilly and Oliver to keep her second identity under wraps, and they have. What good friends! Take this quiz to see how well you can keep your lips sealed.

1. **Your best friend's mother wants to throw a surprise party for her daughter but can't decide what kind of cake to bake. She asks you to find out what flavor your friend is into lately. You ask your friend and she says, "Chocolate. Why do you ask?" You:**
   A. Tell her you're taking a survey for the school paper, then ask the girl at the next desk to make it look official.
   B. Tell her "no reason," then avoid her for the rest of the day. You act so suspicious that she guesses the truth.
   C. Tell her "no reason," but when she keeps asking, finally tell all.

2. **You keep a diary which you write in every night. How many people know about it?**
   A. My parents, my friends . . . everyone.
   B. No one. That's my own personal business.
   C. Just a few select people.

3. Your mom asks you to hide the birthday gift she bought for your brother. You put it:

A. In the back of your closet, in an old shoe box, buried under a mountain of clothing.

B. Under your bed.

C. On your desk. What are the odds he'll spot it there?

4. You overhear a bit of gossip that you know the coolest girl in school would be dying to hear. You:

A. Immediately tell her. She's going to think you're so cool!

B. Keep it to yourself. It's not your place to spread stories.

C. Struggle with it for days, then when you hear *her* talking about it, tell her you totally heard about it days ago.

5. It's April Fool's Day, and you've stuck a whoopee cushion on your best friend's seat in class. She's about to sit down. What happens next?

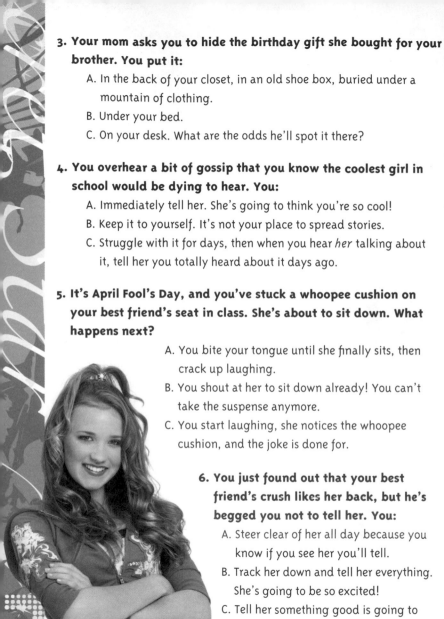

A. You bite your tongue until she finally sits, then crack up laughing.

B. You shout at her to sit down already! You can't take the suspense anymore.

C. You start laughing, she notices the whoopee cushion, and the joke is done for.

6. You just found out that your best friend's crush likes her back, but he's begged you not to tell her. You:

A. Steer clear of her all day because you know if you see her you'll tell.

B. Track her down and tell her everything. She's going to be so excited!

C. Tell her something good is going to happen, but you can't tell her what.

SCORING:

Did You Know?

Miley isn't the only talented singer on *Hannah Montana*. Emily (Lilly) has quite a voice, too. Maybe one day we'll get to hear it on the show.

If you scored:

0–4
Blabbermouth

You should try harder to remember that when people tell you secrets, they're showing they trust you. Telling other people's secrets can ruin friendships, and we don't want that to happen to you!

5–8
Semisecretive

You only tell the really big stuff that nobody could possibly be expected to keep to themselves. Except that someone told you the secret because you promised you would keep it to yourself. Next time you're about to spill the beans, imagine how you would feel if someone told your big secret. Chances are you'll keep quiet, and your friends will love you for it.

9–12
Zipped Lips

Good for you! You're a good secret keeper. Maybe you should look into a career with the CIA! Or maybe you should just keep being the good friend you clearly are. We'd trust you with all our biggest secrets!

Are You Superstar Material?

It takes a special kind of person to be a star. She has to be talented, confident, and able to handle any crazy situations that come her way. Like, you know, Oliver Oken trying to climb through the window of her limousine. Or coming down with poison oak in the middle of a live interview. Or maybe getting handcuffed to her best friend on the night of the Silver Boot Awards. Being Hannah Montana sure is an adventure! Take this quiz to find out if you're confident and cool enough to be a star!

1. You're walking the catwalk during a celebrity fashion show and your heel catches on your gown. You fall down—hard. What do you do?

A. Run off the stage in tears.

B. Get right back up, take a little bow, and keep on walking.

C. Hyperventilate, but eventually get up and finish your walk as quickly as possible.

2. Your history teacher asks you a question in class. She tells you your answer is wrong, but you're sure it's right. What do you do?

A. Raise your hand again and tell her that, actually, you think you're right.

B. Keep your mouth shut. She's the teacher, after all.

C. Double check your book after class and then show it to her. (It's always good to double check.)

3. You're in the middle of singing your solo in the school musical when you completely blank on the words. You:

A. Improvise a few dance moves until the words come back to you, and then keep singing.

B. Hum along to the music and look into the wings for someone—anyone—to shout the words to you and get you going again.

C. Faint. Or pretend to faint. Or do whatever it takes to get you out of it, *now*.

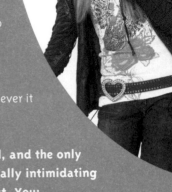

4. There's a new, trendy store in the mall, and the only kids that are ever seen in there are totally intimidating older kids. You're dying to check it out. You:

A. Walk by it ten times nervously before ducking inside and sticking close to the walls.

B. Stride right in. Older kids were your age once, too.

C. Decide to wait until you're a little older to go in.

5. You have a bad case of the sniffles and don't feel like playing in your soccer game this afternoon. Your mother says you have to call your coach and tell her you're sick. You're afraid your coach will give you a hard time since you're a key player. You:

A. Call her right up and explain the situation with no excuses. You know you won't play well if you're feeling under the weather.

B. Call your coach and stutter through a long, tortured explanation about how bad your sniffles are, how sad you are to let the team down, and how you'll be rooting for them from your sickbed.

C. Go to the game. Suffering through sixty minutes of soccer with a stuffed nose is a small price to pay for avoiding a confrontation with your coach.

6. **You're being interviewed on a live, national TV show. As you're answering a question, you let out an enormous burp. The show's host cracks up laughing, and you turn beet red. You:**
   A. Start laughing as well and tell him the burrito you had for lunch clearly didn't agree with you.
   B. Wait until he stops laughing, and then tell him off.
   C. Blush and stammer your way through the rest of the interview. At least you get through it—barely.

7. **As you leave your latest concert by the stage door, twenty screaming fans spot you and chase you to your limousine, begging for autographs. They're a little scary, actually. You:**
   A. Duck into the limo, curl into the corner, and shout at the driver to get out of here.
   B. Duck into the limo, roll the window down a smidge, and sign a few autographs.
   C. Turn around, tell everyone to chill, and then sign autographs and pose for pictures.

SCORING:

1. A-0, B-2, C-1
2. A-2, B-0, C-1
3. A-2, B-1, C-0
4. A-1, B-2, C-0
5. A-2, B-1, C-0
6. A-2, B-0, C-1
7. A-0, B-1, C-2

If you scored:

0-4
Still a Cloud of Cosmic Dust

We're sorry to say it, but if you're dreaming of being a star, you've got a lot of work ahead of you. Hannah's in the public eye all the time, which means she's bound to get into embarrassing situations once in a while, and she always handles them as best she can. You, however, would rather be hiding behind the curtain. Try to work on your confidence. We know you can do it!

5-10
Shooting Star

You're on the track to superstardom! You can usually handle anything that comes up, but sometimes—when life really throws you a curveball—you just hide under the nearest rock. Come on out and show your stuff! You won't be sorry.

11-14
Supernova!

Girl, you so know how to handle yourself. You are not easily embarrassed, and when something humiliating *does* happen to you, you handle it with class. You could give Hannah Montana a run for her money!

R for Revenge

Generally, Miley is a pretty laid-back kind of girl. But every once in a while, mean girls Amber and Ashley do something so ornery that Miley just has to fight back. What about you? Take our quiz to find out if you're a cool, go-with-the-flow girl, or always out for revenge!

1. **You saved up all summer for a hot pair of sunglasses you saw in a magazine. You finally buy the superexpensive shades, and then, two days later, they fall apart. You:**
   A. Write the company a reasonable letter asking that they refund your money or send you a replacement pair of sunglasses.
   B. Cry. A lot. Then go buy a 99-cent pair on the boardwalk.
   C. Write an angry letter to the company, send a copy of the letter to the local paper, and get all your friends to sign a petition saying they'll boycott the company until you're given three pairs of sunglasses (one to replace the broken pair, and two more to make up for how you've suffered).

2. **You come home from school ready to chill out by listening to some music. You find that your younger brother has used all your CDs as Frisbees. You:**
   A. Sigh and clean up the mess, hoping your favorite CDs are okay.
   B. Go to your parents, tell them what happened, and see if they can come up with a way to help you.
   C. Go to his room and destroy his five favorite action figures.

3. **You walk around a corner at school and see your best friend smooching the boy you like. She _knew_ you liked him! You:**

   A. Never talk to her again. Okay, well, not _never_. But you give her the silent treatment for a solid hour, at least.

   B. Forgive her. Clearly he likes her. How can you change that?

   C. Leave something smelly in her locker every day for one month straight.

4. **You forgot to do your chores for the tenth week in a row, so your mom grounds you on the night of the biggest party of the year. (You were warned!) You:**

   A. Purposely forget her birthday. She ruins your night? You'll ruin hers.

   B. Hate it, but deal with it. You know you should have done your chores.

   C. Sulk in your room for an hour, then make a batch of microwave popcorn and suggest you and your mom watch a movie on TV together.

5. The girl who sits next to you in Spanish class cheated off you on the last test, and you both got in trouble since the teacher couldn't tell who cheated off whom. Now you have to do a big project to make up the grade. You:

    A. Let it go and decide you'll do a better job of covering your paper during the next test.

    B. Do the project, but ask if you can move to a different seat. You don't want this to happen again.

    C. Sabotage her extra-credit project. After all, she doesn't deserve the points.

6. One of your friends has a slumber party and doesn't invite you. You:

    A. Have a slumber party and don't invite her.

    B. Figure she had some kind of guest limit and shrug it off.

    C. Have a heart-to-heart talk to find out if she's mad at you for some reason.

SCORING:

1. A-1, B-2, C-0
2. A-2, B-1, C-0
3. A-1, B-2, C-0
4. A-0, B-2, C-1
5. A-2, B-1, C-0
6. A-0, B-2, C-1

Did You Know?

The *Hannah Montana* taping takes place at 4 p.m. on Fridays in Hollywood.

If you scored:

0-4
Revenge is Sweet! Not.

We feel sorry for anyone who has ever crossed you. Whether they took your last piece of gum or stole your best friend, you're going to get back at them. But hurting people just because they hurt you will only make you angry and sad. Instead, try talking to the person who wronged you and see if you can work it out. You'll both be better off.

5-8
Taking Care of Business

You know how to stand up for yourself when someone wrongs you, but you don't stoop to revenge. You're assertive, but you're always ready to work things out and then move on. Kudos—the world needs more people like you!

9-12
Peace, Man

You really know how to let the little things go. And the big things. And everything in between. We admire your calm, cool attitude, but make sure you're not being taken advantage of. When someone wrongs you, speak up. Otherwise, you might end up having people walk all over you. And no one wants that!

Hannah Montana Trivia Quiz #4: Rock the House

You're halfway through our Hannah Montana trivia quizzes, and we've got to say, the crowd is going wild! Now you've got to keep them on their feet, so turn up the amps and pump up the energy as you take on your toughest test yet!

1. **Which of the following actresses plays Miley's mother in a dream sequence?**
   A. Jennifer Aniston
   B. Jennifer Garner
   C. Brooke Shields

2. **In the dream sequence, Jackson is a rock star while Miley has to clean the Stewarts' house. What is Jackson's stage name?**
   A. Texas Timmy
   B. Bucky Kentucky
   C. Corey Missouri

3. **When Miley wins a Silver Boot Award, Lilly has to come along to tape her acceptance speech, even though they're fighting. Why?**
   A. She promised Miley she'd go.
   B. Miley's her ride home.
   C. Oliver has handcuffed them together.

4. What embarrassing object does Miley bring to her first day of high school to help calm her nerves?
   A. Her baby blanket
   B. Her teddy bear
   C. Her favorite dolly

5. Which character tries to blackmail Miley, texting her that he/she knows Miley's secret?
   A. Rico
   B. Jackson
   C. Amber

6. When Lilly gets stood up for a school dance, what do Miley and Lilly do to her date?
   A. Embarrass him in front of the whole school
   B. Take him to teen court
   C. Steal his homework

7. Miley creates a song-and-dance routine to help her remember the facts for a big test at school. What subject is the test on?
   A. Chemistry
   B. Math
   C. Anatomy

ANSWERS:

1. C   5. A
2. B   6. B
3. C   7. C
4. B

SCORING:

Give yourself two points for each correct answer.

If you scored:

0–4 Stage Fright

Nervous, are you? Well, it definitely shows. But don't keep hiding in the wings. Go back to the beginning and see how you do on your second try!

6–10 Backup Dancer

Not bad! Clearly you've been paying attention to Miley and Hannah's latest adventures. You're more than ready to take the stage, but maybe you should support the star for now.

12–14 Spotlight-Worthy

Someone was born to be a star! And that someone is you. You know so much about Hannah, she'd be proud to have you as her opening act anytime. So get out on that stage and work that spotlight!

Did You Know?

"Just Like You" and "The Other Side of Me" were originally tested for the opening theme song, before "The Best of Both Worlds" was chosen.

Are You Image Obsessed?

Miley (as Hannah Montana) once agreed to be in an ad for a zit cream. A photographer took glamorous photos of her to use on the billboard campaign, but the finished ad had a larger-than-life pimple superimposed on her face! Miley was *so* embarrassed!

Lilly helped her friend put it into perspective, reminding Miley that looks don't matter as much as what's inside. It worked! Miley came to appreciate the ad's message: everyone gets zits sometimes—even superstars.

Take our quiz to find out how you feel about *your* looks!

1. **Your hairstylist retired and you have to try out someone new. Problem? The new guy gives you a cut that looks like it was created with a chain saw. You:**
   A. Style it as best you can and go to school. It's just hair. It'll grow.
   B. Wear a hat for two months and claim it's a fashion statement.
   C. Stay at home pretending to be sick for as long as humanly possible.

2. **You have to get braces, and your parents scheduled your orthodontist appointment for the day before class pictures are taken. You:**
   A. Throw a tantrum until they reschedule the appointment *after* class-picture day.
   B. Deal. You're going to have to wear the braces for two years anyway.
   C. Keep your mouth closed for the photo, but practice smiling in the mirror at home until you're used to the sight of your braces.

3. **On the morning of the big graduation dance, you wake up with a huge zit on your nose. You:**
   A. Run to the store and buy every zit cream known to man.
   B. Use some cover-up and smile, smile, smile while you're at the dance.
   C. Stay home. You can't let everyone you know see you looking terrible.

4. **Your best friend gives you a T-shirt with a picture of the two of you on it. You think it's kind of dorky, but she clearly loves it. You:**
   A. Wear it to school the next day. You know it'll make her happy.
   B. "Accidentally" spill grape juice on it so that it's completely ruined.
   C. Wear it the next time you go out with her, but bring a sweater to toss on over it, just in case you bump into anyone you know.

5. **In your most recent softball game, you made the last out by blocking the runner from crossing home plate. Sweet! Of course, the runner also elbowed you in the face by mistake and now you have a huge black eye. You:**
   A. Wear it proudly. Hey, you got it getting the *last out*!
   B. Tell your parents it hurts so badly you need to stay home from school for at least a week (even though it doesn't really hurt that much).
   C. Try covering it up with a cool eye patch or sunglasses.

SCORING:

1. A-2, B-1, C-0
2. A-0, B-2, C-1
3. A-1, B-2, C-0
4. A-2, B-0, C-1
5. A-2, B-0, C-1

If you scored:

0–3
Loving the Mirror!

Here's a guess: You don't go anywhere without a mirror, and you know exactly which colors look best on you. While it's good to take pride in your appearance, it shouldn't be the only thing you value in yourself. Be confident. Let people see the real you, not the one you're trying to create. We're sure they'll like you just the way you are.

4–7
Slightly Self-Conscious

You're not one of those people who spends an hour in front of the mirror every school day, but you also don't like being caught with a zit on the night of a big event. Well, no one does. But you can't let it hold you back from going out and having fun. Here's a little-known fact: if you stay confident and forget that zit is there, most of the people around you will, too.

8–10
Image Schmimmage

Congratulations! You have risen above all those fashion magazines and makeover shows! You think about your hair, clothes, and makeup just enough to look cute, and you don't stress about the occasional image mishap. We couldn't be prouder.

Are You a Hard Worker?

Being Hannah Montana isn't all fun and fabulous parties. Well, a lot of it is. But still! It can be hard work! Between doing her schoolwork and going to all those events and concerts, Miley hardly has any time for herself. But a superstar has to do what a superstar has to do. Take our quiz to see if you could buckle down and do what it takes to make it!

1. **You're scheduled to sing at a sold-out show, but it's outdoors and the rain has kept most everyone away. There are only only fifty soaked kids in the audience, and you dislike rain. You:**

   A. Perform anyway. Your fans came out to see a show, and you're going to give them one!

   B. Tell the stage manager to give the audience free tickets to tomorrow's performance, along with an autographed CD.

   C. Cancel the show. You're not performing in this weather.

2. You have a bad cold, and you're supposed to be appearing on a morning news show to promote your new CD. You:

    A. Take some cold medicine, put on makeup, and go. It's only an hour and then you can go back to bed.

    B. Call up and cancel. You're exhausted, and you can't let your fans see you like this.

    C. Ask if they can reschedule for another day. If they can't, do the show.

3. You're supposed to autograph T-shirts at an event from 7 to 8 p.m. It's 8 now, but there are twenty more people on line. You:

    A. Tell the event organizers to shut it down. You've done your hour.

    B. Hang out long enough to give those last twenty people autographs.

    C. Agree to sign T-shirts for the last twenty people— then end up staying for another hour as more people come up to the table.

4. This weekend, your chore is to clean out the garage. You work all morning and are finally done—then you notice a whole mess of stuff behind your dad's motorcycle. You:

    A. Pretend you never saw it.

    B. Go through most of it, then head for the pool to take a break. You'll finish the job later.

    C. Finish the project. If you're going to do something, you should do it right.

5. **There's a new concept in math class that you just don't get. You spend an hour trying to do your homework, but still can't get it. So frustrating! You:**
   A. Give up. Obviously there's a wall in your brain, and no more math is getting through it.
   B. Ask your older brother, the math genius, to explain it to you.
   C. Keep working until you figure it out, even if it means missing your favorite TV show.

6. **You're recording your new song at the studio and you've gone over the chorus a hundred times. Your throat is getting hoarse, but your producer thinks you need one more take. You:**
   A. Just do it. It's important to get this right.
   B. Say you've sung enough today. It's his job to make it sound good.
   C. Ask for a short break, drink a cup of hot tea to soothe your throat, then go back to the studio to try again.

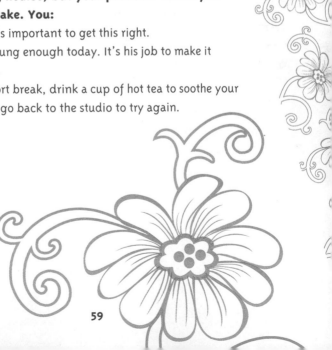

SCORING:

1. A-2, B-1, C-0   4. A-0, B-1, C-2
2. A-2, B-0, C-1   5. A-0, B-1, C-2
3. A-0, B-1, C-2   6. A-2, B-0, C-1

If you scored:

0–3
Lazybones!

Wow! You really value time spent slacking. A lot! You're never going to get anywhere with that attitude! Better get up off the couch and start learning to work hard or you can kiss those pop-star dreams good-bye. In fact, you can kiss any dreams good-bye.

4–8
Easy Does It!

Congrats! You have found the perfect balance between hard work and fun. You know when you have to buckle down and get things done, but you also know that unwinding and chilling out now and then will keep you healthy and happy. You've also figured out that sometimes taking a short break or asking for help from other people can make life a little easier. Good for you!

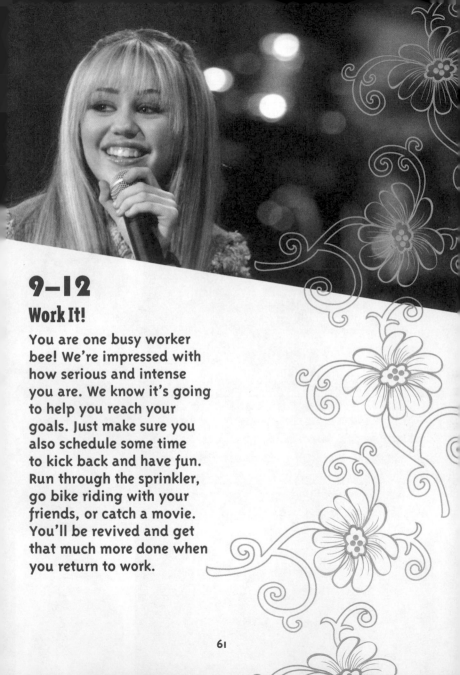

9–12
Work It!

You are one busy worker bee! We're impressed with how serious and intense you are. We know it's going to help you reach your goals. Just make sure you also schedule some time to kick back and have fun. Run through the sprinkler, go bike riding with your friends, or catch a movie. You'll be revived and get that much more done when you return to work.

Could You Handle a Bully?

Unfortunately, bullies are everywhere. We've all run into one at some point in our lives. The question is, do you know how to handle one?

When Miley encounters a bully at her school, her Hannah Montana bodyguard shows up to keep an eye on her. In the end, Miley has to deal with the problem on her own.

Take this quiz to find out whether you could take on a bully without a bodyguard at your back.

1. **You walk out of the lunch line with a tray full of food and some guy takes it right out of your hands. Two seconds later he's scarfing down your spaghetti. You:**

   A. Hope that pack of gum in your purse will hold you until you get home.
   B. Sneak over to his table, grab what you can from your tray, then run.
   C. Tell him to get in line and buy you lunch, since clearly you just bought his.
   D. Find a teacher and tell him or her what happened.

2. **At recess, you see a tough girl bullying a younger kid. You:**
    A. Ignore it. It's none of your business.
    B. Distract her by throwing a basketball near her, giving the kid a chance to run away.
    C. Walk over and tell the girl to pick on someone her own size.
    D. Point out the fight to the nearest grown-up.

3. **The scary new kid in school corners you at your locker and tells you you're going to do her math homework for her. You:**
    A. Do it. It's not worth getting your face rearranged.
    B. Say you'll do it, but don't. Then pretend to be sick so you can stay home the next day and hope for the best.
    C. Tell her no way, and to get out of your face.
    D. Say fine, then tell your math teacher what happened.

4. **A well-known bully is hanging out in the hallway with his friends. You try to get around them, but he trips you. You:**
    A. Get up and walk away.
    B. Laugh and say, "Good one," then scurry away.
    C. Get up and shove the kid.
    D. Go to the principal and report it.

5. **A bully steals your handheld gaming device from your bag and plays it all through lunch. You:**
    A. Hope he has fun with it. You sure did while it was still yours.
    B. Wait until he's distracted by something, then grab it back.
    C. Walk over to his table, grab the device, and tell him to stay out of your stuff.
    D. Report the theft to the principal.

SCORING:

Mostly A's
You are an AVOIDER.

We understand that you're scared, but you can't let people walk all over you. You shouldn't have to be afraid of what's going to happen to you at school. The next time someone tries to take advantage of you, tell an adult.

Mostly B's
You are a TRICKSTER.

We admire that you try to figure a way out of sticky situations. But do you really want to have to constantly figure out yet another tricky move? We didn't think so. Try talking to a trusted teacher or parent about your situation.

Mostly C's
You are a DAREDEVIL.

Okay, so you're brave. But every time you stand up to a bully or get in their face, you run the risk of getting hurt. We're not saying you shouldn't stick up for yourself, but it's probably better to let an adult handle the situation.

Mostly D's
You are a SMART COOKIE.

You've got the right idea! We know a lot of people think that telling an adult about bullying is sort of like tattling, but it's actually the right thing to do. An adult can handle the problem much better than you can, and can help protect you in the process.

Family Matters

Miley's family is superimportant to her. Not only did her father move her whole family from Tennessee to California so that she could pursue her music career, but he is also her manager.

Her brother, Jackson, is always there to drive her where she needs to go and support her when she's down. Okay, sometimes he's there to annoy her, too, but that's what brothers are for.

In return, Miley would do anything for Robby and Jackson. Are you as good to your family as Miley is to hers? Find out with our Family Matters quiz!

1. **It's your little sister's birthday party, and the clown never showed. The kids are freaking out and your sister is near tears. You:**

   A. Go to the beach. You can't stand whiny kids, so you've got to get out of that house!

   B. Throw together the best clown outfit you can come up with and attempt to juggle.

   C. Call every clown in the phone book and see who can get over there fastest.

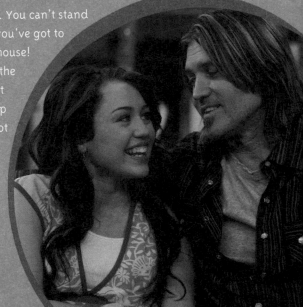

2. **Your father's birthday is coming up, and you always get him a cool present. Problem? You can't think of a new and interesting gift. You:**

A. Brainstorm with your friends until you come up with a cool present idea. You can't let Dad down.

B. Buy him a gift certificate to his favorite store. At least he can pick out something he really wants.

C. Give him a card. He'll understand. Besides, he's too old to care about birthdays anymore.

3. **Your brother, who's a year older than you, likes a girl in your class and asks you to find out if she likes him. You:**

A. Ask the girl. Your brother deserves a girlfriend!

B. Tell him, no way! That's so embarrassing.

C. Advise him to ask her himself. Girls like confident boys, not guys who send their little sisters to do their romancing.

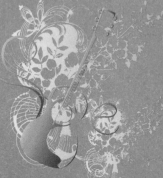

4. **Your mom wants to take you shopping for your prom dress. She's convinced this will be a great bonding experience. Problem? You've already planned to go shopping with your friends. You:**
    A. Tell your mom you'll have to bond some other time.
    B. Invite your mom to come along with you and your friends, knowing that she'll probably get the hint and say no.
    C. Go with your mom. It's important to her, and you know that some day you'll also be glad you have this memory.

5. **It's your weekly family movie night. Your parents have rented a movie you've all been dying to see, but you're in the middle of an IM conversation with your crush. Your parents tell you to come down to the living room already. You:**
    A. Ignore them for as long as possible, then end the conversation and stomp downstairs, pouting.
    B. Tell them you have to skip family movie night this week. There's something important going on here.
    C. Tell your crush you have to go, but you'll IM him tomorrow.

6. **Your mom wants to dress the whole family in matching sweaters for this year's Christmas-card photo. She seems really into the idea, but you'd rather die than risk the chance of your friends seeing you dressed like your parents and sister. You:**
    A. Just do it. It's one picture.
    B. Wear as much jewelry as possible to cover up the sweater.
    C. Tell her you'll do the picture, but only if you don't have to wear the sweater. You have your standards.

SCORING:

1. A-0, B-2, C-1
2. A-2, B-1, C-0
3. A-2, B-0, C-1
4. A-0, B-1, C-2
5. A-1, B-0, C-2
6. A-2, B-1, C-0

If you scored:

0–4
What Family?

You like your family time brief, effortless, and humiliation-free! You're simple and direct about your opinions, even if they hurt feelings. While it's great that you stay true to yourself, you may want to think about how you impact others. You don't need to organize an extralong, family-bonding session every day, but it's worth it to stay up-to-date on each other's lives. You'll feel better knowing your family is on your side, and they'll be comforted knowing you're there for them.

5-8
Family Rocks—Sometimes.

Family is important to you, but you want to have your own identity as well. Members of your family are nowhere near identical, and that works for you. You appreciate each other's tastes (even if they are puzzling). Because you trust your family and they trust you, everyone gets to express themselves freely.

9-12
Family Rules!

Your family members form your strongest support network, and you're always there to encourage, assist, and comfort them. You each share your daily responsibilities as well as the special rewards. Whether you're tackling an unpleasant task or just having some fun, you know life is at its best when you stick together.

Are You True to Yourself?

When Miley loses her singing voice and has to have an operation, she worries that something will go wrong and she'll never get to be Hannah Montana again. Would her friends and family still love her if she was just plain old Miley? She's not so sure, until she has a dream that reminds her that no matter what, Robby, Jackson, Lilly, and Oliver will always love her for her.

Check out our quiz to find out how good you are at just being you.

Did You Know?

Just like Hannah Montana, Miley Cyrus was born in Tennessee.

1. You've always loved astronomy. One day, a popular girl spots you carrying your telescope into school and asks, in a snotty voice, "What's *that* thing?" You say:

   A. "No idea. Some kid asked me to carry it for him."

   B. "It's my telescope. It's really cool; want to check it out?"

   C. "It's a telescope." (Then you walk away. Fast.)

2. You're taking the Presidential Fitness Test in school today, so you're wearing your lucky sneakers. But then you notice how dirty and torn your sneakers are. You:

   A. Wear the sneakers, but you're so self-conscious about them that you do worse than everyone else in the class.

   B. Run to the locker room, throw them out, and dig through the lost and found for a newer pair.

   C. Wear them proudly. They're lucky, after all.

3. You're renting a movie with your three best friends for your slumber party tonight. They grab a movie you all saw together in the theater and say they're just dying to see it again. You, however, hated the movie the first time. You say:

   A. "Ugh. I can't stand that movie! Let's pick something else."

   B. "Omigosh! Yeah! I loved that movie, too!"

   C. "We already saw it. Let's try to find something we haven't seen."

4. **Your grandmother gave you a purple sweater, which you love, for your birthday. When you wear it to school, your best friend says, "Purple is so last year." You:**
   A. Ignore her comment. You like the sweater.
   B. Feel a little self-conscious for the rest of the day.
   C. Wear it until lunch, then change into the sweatshirt you have stashed in your locker.

5. **You love Broadway musicals, and your MP3 player is full of songs from the Great White Way. At lunch, a cute boy checks out your playlist . . . and has a laughing fit when he hears "Put on a Happy Face." You:**
   A. Tell him someone loaded all this weird music on there as a joke.
   B. Tell him he should broaden his horizons. This is good stuff!
   C. Play a more rocking Broadway tune, hoping to convince him how supercool musical theater can be.

6. **You totally love your big old backpack because it can hold all your stuff. But all the other girls at school have these cute little patent leather backpacks. You:**
   A. Head to the mall immediately to buy your own cute little patent leather backpack. You'll figure out how to carry your stuff later.
   B. Keep carrying your old bag. Why fix what's not broken?
   C. Get yourself a patent leather backpack, but only use it on days when you don't have a ton to carry.

SCORING:

1. A-0, B-2, C-1   4. A-2, B-1, C-0
2. A-1, B-0, C-2   5. A-0, B-2, C-1
3. A-2, B-0, C-1   6. A-0, B-2, C-1

If you scored:

0-4
Who ARE You?

You spend so much time listening to what other people think that we're not even sure you know what your opinions are. Stand up for yourself once in a while. Otherwise, you're just going to become a copy of the people around you. And the world would be a boring place if we were all just copies of each other.

5-8
Kinda, Sorta You

Most of the time you're able to stand up for what you believe in and stick to the things you like. But every once in a while, you cave. Like if someone's picking on you a lot, or if you just want to have those cool shoes all the other girls have. That's perfectly natural. Just don't let it happen too often or you might forget who you are. And we think you're pretty cool!

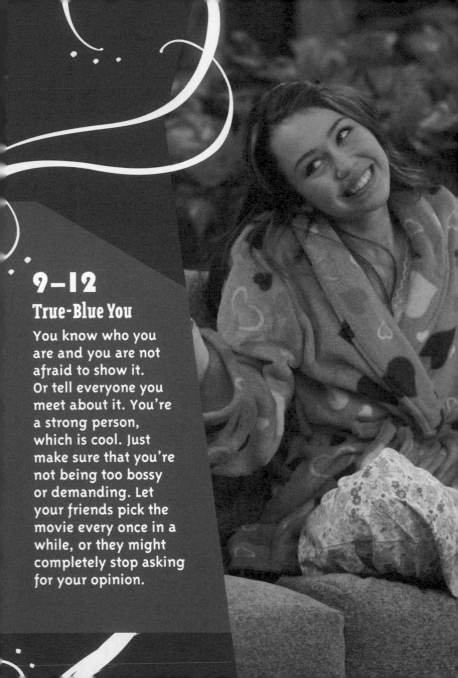

9–12
True-Blue You

You know who you are and you are not afraid to show it. Or tell everyone you meet about it. You're a strong person, which is cool. Just make sure that you're not being too bossy or demanding. Let your friends pick the movie every once in a while, or they might completely stop asking for your opinion.

Hannah Montana Trivia Quiz #5: End on a High Note

Hey, it's almost time to close the show. You need a showstopping last song that will leave the audience yelling for more. Don't get cold feet now, superstar! We know you can do it!

1. How does Miley lose her voice?

    A. Yelling at Jackson

    B. Singing in the shower

    C. Singing six encores at a concert

2. Lilly causes a rift between herself and Miley by choosing her best friend last in what sport?

    A. Kickball

    B. Flag football

    C. Dodgeball

3. Jackson wins tickets to a Lakers game and ends up promising two people the one extra ticket. Which two people think they're going to the game?

    A. Robby and Thor

    B. Robby and Coop

    C. Lilly and Oliver

4. When Miley and Jackson get grounded and sneak out of the house, whose car do they use for their getaway? (Hint: it ends up in a ditch.)

    A. Robby's

    B. Jackson's

    C. Thor's

5. What is the name of Lilly's first real boyfriend?

    A. Jackson

    B. Lucas

    C. Josh

Did You Know?

Miley Cyrus has five siblings. She's right in the middle.

6. **Why does Lilly eventually break up with her first boyfriend?**
    A. She finds out he's cheating on her.
    B. He's annoying.
    C. She finds out he's lying about his age.

7. **When a pair of sunglasses are stolen from Rico's, Rico has a wild security system installed. Who ends up being the shades-stealing criminal?**
    A. Jackson
    B. Oliver
    C. A raccoon

8. **Why does Robby give Jackson the silent treatment?**
    A. Because Jackson never listens when Robby tells him to do his chores.
    B. Because Jackson forgot to get him a birthday present.
    C. Because Jackson unclogged the sink and ended up getting moo shu pork all over Robby in the shower.

ANSWERS:

1. C   5. B
2. B   6. A
3. A   7. C
4. C   8. A

SCORING:

Give yourself two points for each correct answer.

If you scored:

0–4
Your Show Closed Early!

Okay, so you got some answers wrong. Don't feel bad. At least you didn't trip and fall off the stage!

6–10
Take a Bow!

Great job! You know more about Hannah than the average fan. Now it's time to bask in all the applause!

12–16
Standing Ovation!

You couldn't possibly know Hannah Montana better if you *were* Hannah Montana.

Living for the Spotlight

Some people were born to be in the spotlight. Other people just grab the spotlight whenever they get a chance. Miley never thought she was one of those people, until her grandmother came to visit and gave all her attention to Jackson. Then Miley found herself doing everything she could to try to get her grandmother to notice her.

Do you crave attention at all times? And how far would you go to get it? Take our quiz and find out.

1. **The cast list for the winter musical was just posted and you didn't get the lead, but you still landed a good-size part. What's your reaction?**
   A. You're proud of yourself. You congratulate the lead and plan to audition for a bigger part next time.
   B. You're relieved that you didn't get the lead. You're not quite ready to have all eyes on you.
   C. You freak out, screaming and yelling about how wrong it is. You vow to get the lead next time, no matter what!

2. **The school talent show is coming up, and everyone's buzzing about the auditions. What job do you expect to have?**
   A. You'll be the last act. The finale. The one who brings down the house.
   B. You'll have a good number, probably somewhere in the middle of the show.
   C. You'll be backstage, working the lights or handling the curtain.

3. **You're out on the floor with your friends at the Halloween dance when a kid in a mummy costume starts break dancing. Everyone forms a circle around him and starts cheering. You:**
   A. Join the crowd and clap along to the music.
   B. Wait until he's done, then take the center of the circle to dance with one of your friends.
   C. Bust into the circle and show him how it's done.

4. **A girl in your class fell off her bike and broke her arm. When she shows up at school in her pink cast, everyone wants to sign it. You:**
   A. Start loudly reminding everyone about that time you broke your leg and how huge *that* cast was.
   B. Grab a red marker and write a nice note.
   C. Let everyone else sign the cast before you, then lose your chance when the bell rings and everyone has to go to class.

5. **Your class is doing a fashion show fund-raiser and you've drawn straws to see who gets to pick their outfit for the show first. You won! Backstage there are tons of beautiful gowns. You choose:**
   A. The one that suits you best.
   B. The biggest, most colorful, most glittery one.
   C. Whatever the show's organizer recommends.

6. **During rehearsals for the holiday pageant, the star angel develops a fear of heights and resigns her position. What do you do?**
   A. Immediately grab the director and volunteer to take her place.
   B. Try to talk her back up there. If she quits, she'll regret it.
   C. Wait to see what happens, but sing her song to yourself so that the director might overhear how good you are.

7. How often do you raise your hand in class?

    A. Never. What if I gave the wrong answer?

    B. Sometimes. Only if I know I'm right.

    C. Always. Even if I get it wrong, I know I can at least get a laugh.

Did You Know?

Miley's favorite sport is cheerleading, and her favorite hobby is shopping.

SCORING:

1. A-1, B-0, C-2
2. A-2, B-1, C-0
3. A-0, B-1, C-2
4. A-2, B-1, C-0
5. A-1, B-2, C-0
6. A-2, B-0, C-1
7. A-0, B-1, C-2

If you scored:

0 – 4
Standing in the Shadows

Not only do you never go after the spotlight, you'd rather not go anywhere near it. Content to sit on the sidelines or work backstage, no star ever has to worry about you backstabbing her for her role—and that's totally fine. But try to come out of the shadows every once in a while and show the world that you can shine brightly. We don't want anyone to forget you're there.

5–9
Loving the Light
You like to be in the spotlight as much as anyone, but you would never try to steal it from someone else. You're all about earning your place in the sun through hard work and patience—not by grabbing it and pulling it away from others. We like the way you operate.

10–14
Spotlight Hog!
You never met a spotlight you didn't try to claim for your own. But did you ever stop and let someone else shine for a few minutes? We're all for ambition, but don't step on too many toes as you climb the ladder of success. Otherwise, no one will be around to catch you if you happen to fall.

My Way or the Highway!

Miley thought Josh was the coolest guy ever . . . until she found out that he didn't like Hannah Montana's music! How could she possibly like someone who didn't appreciate one of the most important things in her life? So she tried her best to change his mind about Hannah—and failed miserably.

Have you and your friends ever disagreed on something important? If it happened, how would you handle it? Would you try to change them, or would you just accept your differences? Well, you don't have to answer, because we've got the answer for you. Take our quiz and find out how accepting you are.

1. **For ten years, you and your sister always wore matching bathing suits. This year, she suddenly decides she wants something different. What do you do?**

   A. Tell her you won't go to the beach with her this year unless she wears a matching suit.

   B. Wheedle to get your own way by telling her how cute you guys will look in flowered tankinis.

   C. Shrug and pick out your own suit. It's the end of an era, which is sad, but sometimes things change.

2. **Your dad lands concert tickets for the band that you and your best friend have loved forever. When you tell her, she says she's not into that band anymore. You:**

   A. Are disappointed, but understand. You'll take another friend.

   B. Sing her favorite song to remind her of how much she loved them, until she caves.

   C. Say you have no idea who she is anymore and storm out.

3. **It's time to sign up for clubs and teams for the new school year. You're dying to join the environmental club. Your best friend wants to join the photography club. Both clubs meet at the same time. What do you do?**

   A. Explain why you think the environment is an important cause, but accept it if she still wants to check out photography.

   B. Let it go. It's cool that you like different things. It makes you more interesting.

   C. Make her feel guilty about joining the photography club every chance you get.

4. **You and your brother are making breakfast for your mom on Mother's Day. He swears she'll love pancakes, but you know her favorite breakfast is oatmeal. What do you do?**

   A. Let him have his way. You know your mother will be pleased by the thought, anyway.
   B. Make both and see which one she likes better.
   C. Tell him you know what you're doing and he should get out of the kitchen.

5. **Every Saturday you and your friends hit the Burger Barn for burgers and fries. This week one of them suggests you go to the Salad Shack instead and try something different. You can't stand salad. You:**

   A. Agree to go to the Salad Shack and then swing by Burger Barn afterward.
   B. Say, "No way, no how." You have a tradition and you're sticking to it.
   C. Say, "That's fine," and try to find something on the menu you like.

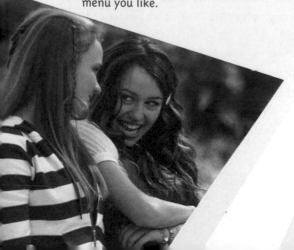

SCORING:

1. A-0, B-1, C-2
2. A-2, B-1, C-0
3. A-1, B-2, C-0
4. A-2, B-1, C-0
5. A-1, B-0, C-2

If you scored:

0–3
Bossy Boots

Right, so does anyone other than you ever have a good idea? Because you don't always act like it. Sometimes you have to try new things and understand that other people can have opinions, too.

4–7
Master Mediator

You like it when everyone agrees with you, but you're okay when they don't. You listen to other people's suggestions and try to come up with a solution that will make everyone happy. Good for you!

8–10
Meek and Mild

When was the last time you stood up for what you wanted? You should give it a try sometime. It's great that you accept your friends for who they are. But are you letting them know who *you* are? You should have your way once in a while, too!

What's Your *Hannah Montana* Theme Song?

Have you worn out your *Hannah Montana* CD from playing it too many times? Yeah, we thought so. We know you've got all the lyrics memorized and have probably choreographed dance routines to every last one of them, but do you know which Hannah song is *your* theme song? Take this quiz to find out which Hannah tune was written for you!

1. **What's the biggest secret you're keeping right at this very moment?**
   - A. I have so many secrets I couldn't pick one.
   - B. Secrets? I have no secrets. I tell everyone exactly what I think.
   - C. I have a secret crush. So romantic!

2. **There's a big dance coming up at school. You can't wait. You just know you:**
   - A. Are going to have the best time dancing with all your friends.
   - B. Are going to be the center of attention.
   - C. Are going to slow dance with the boy of your dreams.

3. **Time for a college-interview question! Where do you want to be in ten years?**
   A. You'll have a supercool job, plus an amazing family to come home to.
   B. You'll be traveling the world on your own, doing whatever you want, whenever you want.
   C. Hanging out with the guy of your dreams. Wherever you are, as long as you're together, that'll be home.

4. **You and your friends are going out on Saturday night but haven't decided what you're going to do yet. There are all kinds of choices. You vote for:**
   A. A concert. Someplace you and your friends can dance and sing and have a great time.
   B. An amusement park. You love a good thrill ride.
   C. A romantic comedy film. You love to lose yourself in love.

SCORING:

Mostly A's

Your theme song is "BEST OF BOTH WORLDS"!

For you, life is about having a good time. Whether you're in Miley mode or Hannah land, it's all about making the best of where you are. You're tons of fun to be around and always bring the party with you!

Mostly B's

Your theme song is "I GOT NERVE"!

Nobody wants to mess with you, because you'll tell them exactly what you think. You stand up for yourself and your friends, and you never turn down a dare. Being around you is like being on a constant roller coaster. You never know what might happen next!

Mostly C's

Your theme song is "IF WE WERE A MOVIE"!

You're all about the romance. You see every party, dance, and day at the beach as a potential setting for the most romantic moment of your life. What a rosy way to live!

Hannah Montana Trivia Quiz #6: Encore! Encore!

This is it! You've put on a great show and the crowd is cheering for more. This is your last chance to leave it all on the stage and show 'em what you've got! Go for it!

1. **What does Oliver wear under his clothes on the first day of high school?**
   A. A Superman outfit
   B. Fake muscles
   C. Polka-dot underwear

2. **In Miley's dream about her mother, what does Miley claim Jackson's singing voice sounds like?**
   A. A starving walrus
   B. A dying monkey
   C. A sick giraffe

3. **When Robby tries to solve an argument between Miley and Jackson by making them fight in padded suits, what do they call him?**
   A. Dr. Daddy
   B. Dr. Phil-Billy
   C. Dr. Robby Ray

4. **What does Oliver Oken's mother do for a living?**
   A. She's a teacher.
   B. She's a mayor.
   C. She's a police officer.

5. Which song wins Hannah her very first Silver Boot Award (or "Booty")?

    A. "I Got Nerve"

    B. "Best of Both Worlds"

    C. "True Friend"

6. Which of the following characters has Miley kissed on the lips?

    A. Jake

    B. Rico

    C. Both

7. When Miley invites Lilly over for a girl's movie night, Lilly brings along her boyfriend, Lucas. Who does she bring along as a date for Miley?

    A. Oliver Oken

    B. Lucas's friend Derek

    C. Lucas's cousin Dex

8. Miley has never been good at sports. The other girls in her gym class call her what nasty nickname because of her lack of talent?

    A. Stinky Stewart

    B. Smelly Miley

    C. Talent-less Tennessee

ANSWERS:

1. B
2. A
3. B
4. C
5. C
6. C
7. B
8. A

SCORING:

Give yourself two points for each correct answer.

If you scored:

0–4
Fizzling Star
Well, you gave it your all, but your encore fizzled in the end. Still, you put on a great show!

6–10
Stage-Worthy
You definitely know how to work a stage! Not only have you got the crowd cheering, but they're thirsty for more.

12–16
Superstar!
Better get used to a life full of red carpets, screaming fans, and stalking paparazzi. You were clearly born to be a star.